For all the children of the world
who dare to see things
as they really are
—Demi

Margaret K. McElderry Books
An imprint of Simon & Schuster Children's
Publishing Division
1230 Avenue of the Americas
New York, New York 10020

Book design by Ann Bobco
The text of this book is set in Centaur.
Hand lettering by Jeanyee Wong
The illustrations were rendered in paint and ink.

Printed in Hong Kong
2 4 6 8 10 9 7 5 3 1

Library of Congress Cataloging-in-Publication Data:
Demi.
The emperor's new clothes/a tale set in China
told by Demi.
p.   cm.
Summary: Two rascals sell a vain Chinese emperor
an invisible suit of clothes.
ISBN 0-689-83068-8
[1. Fairy tales.] I. title.
PZ8.D379Ch   2000   [Fic]—dc21   99-24883

FIRST
EDITION

THE EMPEROR'S NEW CLOTHES

A TALE SET IN CHINA TOLD BY
DEMI

Margaret K. McElderry Books

Long ago in a province in China, there lived an emperor

whose greatest pleasure in life was to dress in new clothes.

Day and night in the winter, the
palace spinners spun skeins of the
smoothest silk and the warmest wool.

Day and night in the summer, the palace weavers wove cloth of the lightest linen and the coolest cotton.

Day and night all year long, the palace tailors sewed gowns and tunics and trousers and scarves.

And every few hours of every day, the palace dressers
dressed the Emperor in a new set of clothes so that he might
walk proudly among his people and be admired.

One fall day, two strangers—a woman and a man—
arrived in the province. They claimed to be the finest weaver
and the finest tailor who ever lived. They were brought
before the Emperor.

"Your Imperial Highness," the strangers said, "we have
come to offer you clothes that no one else in the world has
ever had."

The Emperor was intrigued. "What kind of clothes can
these be?" he asked.

"Clothes that are not only beautiful to see and touch, but
clothes that are woven and tailored with magic," said the woman.

"Magic?" the Emperor asked.

"The clothes we make are so magical that only clever people can see them. Fools cannot," replied the man.

"I must have those clothes!" the Emperor declared. "I can wear them and see who in the province is clever and who is a fool! You must make them for me at once!"

So the woman and the man were paid and set up in the palace in their own workroom. And they asked not to be disturbed.

SWASTIKA
happiness

COIN
wealth

PEACH
immortality

PEAR
purity

POMEGRANATE
posterity

CITRON
wealth

After a while, when the land was frozen under winter ice and snow, the Emperor became curious about his new magical clothes. He sent his Imperial Minister to check on the progress of the weaver and the tailor.

When the Imperial Minister arrived in the workroom, the weaver was hunched over her empty loom and the tailor was snapping his scissors through the air.

The Imperial Minister couldn't be called a fool, so he told the Emperor that the cloth he'd seen was the most beautiful and luxurious imaginable. He pretended he had seen cloth more magical than the plumage of a bird.

"Isn't this the finest cloth you've ever seen?" asked the woman.

"Isn't this the most delicate brocade you've ever touched?" asked the man.

The Imperial Minister was alarmed. Was he a fool? He could see nothing at all!

The Emperor was delighted with the Minister's report. After a while, when the land was glowing again with spring, the Emperor became impatient about his new magical clothes. He sent his High Chancellor to check on the progress of the weaver and the tailor.

When the High Chancellor arrived in the workroom, the weaver was struggling to carry a load of air and the tailor was sewing something with neither needle nor thread.

"Isn't this the most splendid fabric you've ever touched?" asked the woman.

"Isn't this the most glorious design you've ever seen?" asked the man.

The High Chancellor was astonished. Was he a fool? He could see nothing at all!

He couldn't be called a fool, so the High Chancellor told the Emperor that the garments he'd touched were the most graceful and exquisite garments imaginable. He pretended that the clothing he'd seen was more magical than the colors of the rainbow.

The Emperor was shocked. Was he a fool? He could see nothing at all!

He certainly couldn't be called a fool!

He took off his clothes and pretended to put on the splendid new clothing one piece at a time. Then he turned and preened in front of the mirror. "My new outfit is more magical than all the stars in the sky!" he said.

The Emperor was overjoyed with the Chancellor's report.

After a while, when the land was burning under the summer sun, the Emperor decided to see the new magical clothes for himself.

The Emperor, the High Chancellor, and the Imperial Minister arrived in the workroom.

The weaver curtsied and held up a hanger.

"Your Highness, look at the colors!"

cried the Imperial Minister.

The tailor bowed and held out his arms.

"Your Highness, look at the style!"

exclaimed the High Chancellor.

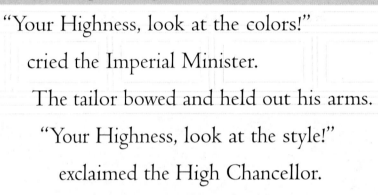

The Emperor walked out into the province.

The people were surprised. Were they fools?

Their Emperor was wearing nothing at all!

The people did not want to be called fools.
"Doesn't His Highness look divine in those fine fabrics?"
they asked one another. "Don't the colors of
his clothes shimmer? Doesn't he look like a star?"

The Emperor decided to walk
among his people and be admired.

The Imperial Minister and the
High Chancellor dared not admit they
could see nothing on their Emperor,
and they prepared to accompany him
on his walk.

"But he has nothing on!" a child called out.

"The Emperor has no clothes!"

The Emperor heard the child.

He knew who the fools were in his province.

But he held his head high and continued to walk among his people.

AUTHOR'S NOTE

In early China, painting was regarded as an art of magic. Painters, through their creative powers, were magicians. These magicians were keen observers of life whose spirit came from a deep conviction that every phenomenon of life—from the tiny ant and the lowly stone to the royal emperor and the majestic mountain—was made up of *ch'i*, the essence of life.

In the Chinese concept of *ch'i*, everything one paints relates to Heaven—and so in this version of *The Emperor's New Clothes*, I have used the color gold, which is the color of purity. The Chinese symbols used throughout the illustrations are reminders of all aspects of purity in life. In the winter scene outside the palace, the New Year's celebration is an act of purification for the days ahead, and the Chinese dragon is the symbol of pure wealth, wisdom, and power. In the spring scene outside the palace, the process of weaving silk from silkworms symbolizes delicate purity and virtue. The summertime kite-flying outside the palace echoes the idea that a sure way to reach Heaven is to write your purest wishes on a kite and send them soaring on the wind.

Though he is surrounded by elements of purity and virtue, the Emperor in this story doesn't have the courage of his own convictions to admit the truth about his invisible clothing. It takes a child—whose voice is that of innocence and truth—to bring wisdom to the Emperor, enabling him to fill his role as representative of Heaven on Earth.

In painting the pictures for *The Emperor's New Clothes*, I have tried to capture the magic that is China by including elements of Chinese culture in each picture, and to circulate the *ch'i* that is in all things for young readers to share.

Demi